SIMON & SCHUSTER CHILDREN'S PUBLISHING

ADVANCE READER'S COPY

TITLE: A Shai & Emmie Story: Shai & Emmie Star in Break an Egg!

AUTHOR: Quvenzhané Wallis with Nancy Ohlin

ILLUSTRATOR: Sharee Miller

IMPRINT: Simon & Schuster Books for Young Readers

ON-SALE DATE: 10/3/17

ISBN: 978-1-4814-5882-5

FORMAT: hardcover

PRICE: $15.99/$21.99 CAN

AGES: 6-10

PAGES: 128

Please send two copies of any review or mention of this book to:
Simon & Schuster Children's Publicity Department
1230 Avenue of the Americas, 4th Floor
New York, NY 10020
212/698-2808

Aladdin • Atheneum Books for Young Readers
Beach Lane Books • Beyond Words • Libros para niños
Little Simon • Margaret K. McElderry Books
Paula Wiseman Books • Salaam Reads •
Simon & Schuster Books for Young Readers
Simon Pulse • Simon Spotlight

To my family, friends, and fans,
for the love and continuous support
—Q. W.

To my mother, who always made it possible
for me to do what I love
—S. M.

SIMON & SCHUSTER BOOKS FOR YOUNG READERS
An imprint of Simon & Schuster Children's Publishing Division
1230 Avenue of the Americas, New York, New York 10020
For information about special discounts for bulk purchases, please contact
Simon & Schuster Special Sales at 1-866-506-1949 or business@simonandschuster.com.
The Simon & Schuster Speakers Bureau can bring authors to your live event. For more information or to book an event,
contact the Simon & Schuster Speakers Bureau at 1-866-248-3049 or visit our website at www.simonspeakers.com.
Book design by Chloë Foglia • The text for this book was set in Bembo.
The illustrations for this book were rendered in watercolor and ink.
Manufactured in the United States of America
0917 FFG
First Edition
2 4 6 8 10 9 7 5 3 1
Library of Congress Cataloging-in-Publication Data
Names: Wallis, Quvenzhané, 2003– author. | Ohlin, Nancy, author. | Miller, Sharee (Illustrator), illustrator.
Title: Shai & Emmie star in Break an egg! : a Shai & Emmie story /
Quvenzhané Wallis with Nancy Ohlin ; Illustrated by Sharee Miller.
Other titles: Shai and Emmie star in Break an egg!
Description: First edition. | New York : Simon & Schuster Books for Young Readers, [2017] | Summary: When Shai Williams,
who plans to become a star on Broadway, loses the lead role in the third-grade musical at her performing arts elementary
school in Atlanta, she learns an important lesson about adaptability, from her mother, aunt, and grandmother, all actresses.
Identifiers: LCCN 2016005374| ISBN 9781481458825 (hardcover : alk. paper) | ISBN 9781481458849 (ebook)
Subjects: | CYAC: Theater—Fiction. | Acting—Fiction. | Friendship—Fiction. |
Schools—Fiction. | African Americans—Fiction.
Classification: LCC PZ7.1.W357 Sh 2017 | DDC [Fic]—dc23
LC record available at https://lccn.loc.gov/2016005374

Shai & Emmie
STAR IN
BREAK AN EGG!

Quvenzhané Wallis

WITH Nancy Ohlin

ILLUSTRATED BY Sharee Miller

Program

SCENE 1

The New Girl

Shai Williams slipped on her sunglasses and strolled into drama class.

"Please, no photos!" she said in her best movie-star voice. She believed in making an entrance.

Everyone cracked up . . . except for a girl in a green sundress who just looked confused. Shai had never seen her before. Who was she, anyway?

"*Shai!*" Emmie Harper, Shai's best friend,

stage-whispered. "Stage-whispering" was something Ms. Gremillion had taught them in class last week. It meant whispering kind of loudly—like the way Shai's parents did whenever she got restless in church or slipped food to Sugar under the table.

Shai took the seat next to Emmie. As she set her turquoise backpack on the floor, her rhinestone initials glittered in the sunlight—*SRW*, for Shaianne Rosa Williams. "Shaianne" was pronounced "Shay-Anne," although it often got mispronounced as "Shy-Anne." Still, Shai loved her name, which was a mash of her parents' names, "Shaquille" and "Annemarie."

"Nice entrance," Emmie said, complimenting her.

"Thanks," Shai stage-whispered. "Who's that girl in the green dress?"

"She's new. Libby heard a rumor that she's

a professional actor," replied Emmie.

Shai whipped off her sunglasses. "Excuse me?"

"Libby thinks she's been on TV. Oh, and guess what else she heard?"

Emmie continued to talk, but Shai had

stopped listening. She was still stuck on the part about the new girl being a professional actor.

The Sweet Auburn School for the Performing Arts was all about becoming a professional actor or a musician or a dancer . . . *someday*. It was an elementary school for kindergarten through fifth grade, and Shai and the other students were just starting to learn those performance skills.

So, what was a professional actor doing here? "Professional" meant having jobs; it meant already having serious acting skills.

"—*on This Island*! Wouldn't that be amazetastic?" Emmie was saying.

"It's not like I'm jealous or anything. Besides, it's just a rumor, so it's probably not even true," Shai said with a shrug.

"Huh? Shai, did you hear what I just said? About the third-grade musical?"

Ms. Gremillion walked into the room just as the bell rang. The students fell silent and pulled their notebooks and pens out of their backpacks.

"Good afternoon, boys and girls," said Ms. Gremillion.

"Good afternoon, Ms. Gremillion!"

Ms. Gremillion paused dramatically and scanned the room. "Dramatic pauses" had been another recent lesson. It meant being quiet in an interesting way so that your audience listened carefully to whatever you said next.

"Before we begin, I want to make two quick announcements," she said. "First, our musical this year will be *Once on This Island*. If you're interested in trying out, the auditions will be this Friday."

Emmie grinned. "See, I *told* you!" she stage-whispered to Shai.

Shai jumped to her feet. She couldn't help it—she was really excited! *Once on This Island* was one of her favorite musicals.

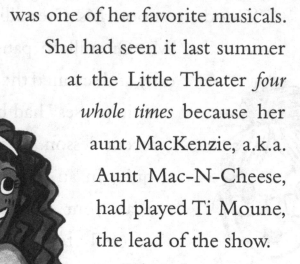

She had seen it last summer at the Little Theater *four whole times* because her aunt MacKenzie, a.k.a. Aunt Mac-N-Cheese, had played Ti Moune, the lead of the show.

"Shai, do you have something you'd like to share?" asked Ms. Gremillion.

"Yes! I mean, no! I

mean, I want to try out for Ti Moune!" Shai blurted out.

"That's great, Shai," Ms. Gremillion said.

The new girl sat up very straight and gave a little wave.

Ms. Gremillion nodded at her. "Yes, Gabby, you're my second announcement. Class, this is Gabrielle Supreme. She and her family just moved here from Los Angeles, California."

"Hollywood, actually," Gabby said as she flipped her hair.

Hollywood? Shai scrunched up her face so hard that her nose hurt. Hollywood was where they made movies and TV shows.

So maybe Gabby was a professional actor after all?

Not that Shai was jealous or anything.

In any case, there was no way Ms. Hollywood was going to replace Shai as the best actor in the third grade. Did Gabby own a shiny gold trophy that said FUTURE OSCAR WINNER? An Oscar was one of the biggest awards in the acting world. Granted, Shai's family had given her the trophy for her birthday, but so what?

The new girl didn't stand a chance.

SCENE 2

Penelope Periwinkle's Guide to Great Acting

Shai sat cross-legged on her bed, reading *Penelope Periwinkle's Guide to Great Acting*. Sugar was curled up next to her, thumping her tail and blinking her big brown eyes. She looked super-cute in a sequined ballet tutu and polka-dot hair ribbon.

Penelope Periwinkle's Guide to Great Acting was an amazetastic book packed with useful information about acting. Shai had found it at the bookstore last month and had bought it with her allowance money.

The book would help her win the role of Ti Moune—not that she needed a lot of help in that department. She already knew Ti Moune's part really well because of Aunt Mac-N-Cheese. Also, she had tons of stage experience. Last year she'd played nasty old Miss Hannigan in *Annie*. The year before, she'd played Ray in *The Princess and the Frog*.

Shai took her craft seriously—she wanted to be a movie star when she grew up. And a dentist, too, because she thought teeth were cool. Plus maybe a veterinarian like her mom. Her dad, who owned a pizza restaurant, liked to call her a "triple threat in the making" because of her three future careers.

Mostly, though, she wanted to be a movie star, and Penelope Periwinkle had lots of smart advice about that.

Shai turned to the chapter about breathing.

A Great Actor must have excellent breath control, stated Penelope Periwinkle.

Shai took a couple of quick, panting breaths, like Sugar did whenever she wanted a Bitty Bites puppy treat. Shai pictured herself as Ti Moune, breathing very excellently as she rescued Daniel, the wealthy boy from the other side of the island, during a terrible rainstorm.

To develop your breath, try this exercise. Lie down on a flat surface. Place something light on your stomach.

Shai glanced around her room. Her lava lamp? *Too heavy.* Her dinosaur tooth collection? *Not heavy enough.*

Her gaze landed on Sugar. *Hmm.*

Shai reached over and picked up the little Morkie. She lay back on her satiny turquoise bedspread and balanced Sugar on her stomach. She held up the book with both hands.

Breathe in and out deeply and slowly, Penelope Periwinkle instructed.

Shai breathed in and out deeply and slowly. Sugar blinked at her.

As you breathe, watch the object on your stomach go up and down, up and down.

Sugar went up and down, up and down.

The next time you breathe out, say, "Ahhhhhh!"

"Ahhhhhh!" said Shai.

"Woof!" barked Sugar.

Now breathe out the sound "Eeeeeee!"

"Eeeeeee!" said Shai.

"Woof!" barked Sugar.

Breathe out the sound "Ooooooo!"

"Ooooooo!" said Shai.

"Woof!" barked Sugar.

The door opened, and Patches trotted into the room. Patches was part collie and part German shepherd and part a bunch of other things. She squatted by the bed and stared up at Shai and Sugar. "Aooooooo!" she howled.

A few seconds later Noodle the Poodle came in too. "Aooooooooo!" he howled.

Soon all five dogs were in the room howling, Sugar included. Shai's family had a lot of pets because Momma was always bringing home strays from the veterinary clinic.

"You guys are interrupting my process!" Shai scolded them.

"Whatcha doing, Shai-Shai?"

Her little sister, Samantha, stood in the doorway swinging her purple dragon, Mr. Firebreath, by the tail. She had dressed him up in a tiny doll apron and baby booties.

"Are you conductoring a dog orchestra?" Samantha asked.

"*Conducting*. And, no—I'm practicing for a very, very important audition. Didn't you see the sign on my door?"

Shai made a stern-teacher face and pointed to the piece of paper taped to her door. She had scribbled "DO NOT DISTURB" on it in big letters. But someone had covered most of the letters with shark and princess stickers. Only the *U* and *R* and *B* were visible.

Jacobe had struck again. . . .

"Urb," Shai grumbled.

"What's the addition for? Can I addition too?" asked Samantha.

"*Audition.* And, no, you can't. You're too little."

"I am *not* too little. I'm five and one quarter!"

"It's the *third-grade* musical."

"So? Kindergarten is *almost* third grade!"

"Kids! Time to wash up for dinner!" their dad called up the stairs.

Footsteps pounded down the hall. Jacobe ran by Shai's doorway wearing nothing but a diaper and a feather boa. Their older brother, Jamal, chased after him. One of the marmalade kitties, either Purrball or Furball, trailed after Jamal. The dogs scrambled out of Shai's room and followed the group, yipping and barking.

"Daddy! Are we having 'paghetti with red sauce for dinner? Can I have super-duper-quadruple Parmesan cheese?" Samantha shouted.

Shai squeezed her eyes shut and covered

her ears. How was she supposed to study Great Acting with all this noise?

And then she remembered something Penelope Periwinkle had written in chapter one.

A Great Actor must be able to focus even through chaos.

Shai nodded to herself, feeling very wise. "Chaos" was crazy stuff happening all at once. Chaos hadn't kept Ti Moune from being a brave heroine. Chaos wouldn't keep Shai from being a Great Actor . . . a *super-duper-quadruple* Great Actor.

SCENE 3

Toothpaste and Zombies

On Wednesday, Ms. Gremillion had a special acting lesson for the class.

"Today you will be improvising scenes with a partner," she explained.

Shai caught Emmie's eye across the aisle. She mouthed, *Partners?*

Emmie grinned and gave her a wiggly two-thumbs-up. *Partners!*

Gabby sat up front near Ms. Gremillion. As the teacher started the lesson, Gabby began taking careful notes in a glittery green note-book and doing a lot of hair-flipping. Shai frowned and began writing in her notebook too. She didn't want Ms. Gremillion to think she wasn't a good attention-payer.

She wrote:

"We're going to start with an *unstructured* improvisation exercise. Can anyone tell me what we mean by 'unstructured improvisa-tion'?" Ms. Gremillion asked.

Rio Garcia raised his hand. Shai would have raised her hand, except that she was too busy drawing exclamation marks and smiley faces in her notebook. Plus, she had no idea what "unstructured improvisation" meant.

"Yes, Rio?"

"Well, 'structured' means that something is organized. And 'improvisation' is making stuff up, like scenes. So 'unstructured improvisation' means making up scenes in a not-organized way?"

"That's right. With *structured* improvisation there's a prompt or direction, like, 'improvise a birthday party scene.' With *unstructured* improvisation there are no prompts or directions. One partner just starts acting, and the other partner has to respond on the spot."

Funsies! Shai thought. She and Emmie already did this anyway. Just that morning in science she had pretended to be bacteria while Emmie had pretended to be an amoeba.

Ms. Gremillion peered around the room. "Libby, you'll partner up with Julia. Ben, you're with Nick. Let's see . . . then Ruby and Garrett, Nya and Sarah, Glenn and Jay, Molly and Isabella,

Capone and Ezra, Rio and Emmie. That leaves Gabby and Shai."

Wait, what? Shai thought. Did Ms. Gremillion just pair her up with Gabby? It had to be a mistake. She and Emmie were *always* partners.

She raised both hands so that she could get her teacher's double attention. "Ms. Gremillion? Did you mean *Emmie* and me?"

"No, Shai. I meant Gabby and you, Emmie and Rio."

Emmie made a pouty face at Shai. Shai made a pouty face back. She felt a secret twinge of worry, too. What if Gabby was better at this unstructured improvisation business than she was?

"Partners, please get together and decide who'll go first," said Ms. Gremillion. "Partner number one will think of a character to play and improvise some dialogue. Partner number two will improvise back. Got it?"

Gabby pranced up to Shai. "I guess we're partners!" she said with a big smile.

"Yup, I guess we are." Shai forced herself to smile back. Gabby didn't seem too scary up close. Shai thought about something her grandma Rosa often said: "Have the courage to be nice to people." Maybe Shai should make an effort to be nice. She could do "nice" really well; she was an actor, after all.

Although . . . what did courage have to do with being nice? She reminded herself to ask Grandma Rosa about that.

"So! Gabby! Welcome to our school! How do you like it so far?"

"Meh. It's okay for a small-town school. Have you ever done unstructured improvisation?"

A small-town school? "Um, no. Have you?"

"Of course. I'd better go first, then, since you're just a beginner."

Just a beginner?

Gabby closed her eyes and squeezed her hands into fists. Then she opened her eyes and flung her arms out wide, almost knocking down a music stand.

"Mother, you cannot hold me back!" Gabby said in a loud, dramatic voice. "It is my dream—my destiny!—to move to New York City and become a Broadway star!"

Shai stared at Gabby. *Seriously?* Still, she had to admit that Gabby had delivered her weird lines really well.

"That's your cue, Shane," Gabby stage-whispered.

"It's *Shai*."

"Whatever."

Shai closed her eyes and squeezed her hands into fists too. She took a bunch of deep breaths. She would show Gabby that she was a Great Actor, not a beginner.

"Ahhhhh," Shai breathed. "Eeeee. Ooooo."

"Huh?" said Gabby in her regular Gabby voice. Then she switched to her drama voice. "I mean . . . Mother, are you ill?"

"Broadway just called," Shai improvised, "and they want me, not you. So you're going to stay behind and take over our family's cat litter company!"

"*What?*"

"I must go pack for my trip now. Good luck with the cat litter!"

"But—"

Ms. Gremillion blew a whistle. "Okay, class. Take a sixty-second break, then switch places with your partner, please!"

Shai and Gabby turned to face each other.

"Nice work, *Shane*," Gabby said in a fakey-sweet way.

"You too, *Grabby*!" Shai said in an even faker, sweeter way.

"Hey, Shane! Are you really trying out for the part of Ti Moune? You might want to think about trying out for an easier part. Like maybe one of the forest animals?"

"Excuse me?"

"Besides, I'm trying out for Ti Moune too. I'll probably get it because I have *tons* of acting experience. Did you know I was in a movie? I played a talking french fry in *The Attack of the Zombie Potatoes 4.* And I was one of the singing teeth in the Smile More toothpaste commercial."

Shai opened her mouth, but no words came out. Grabby Gabby wanted the role of Ti Moune too. And it turned out she really *was* a professional actor.

Would Shai be able to compete against that?

SCENE 4

Not Freaking Out

"Gabby is *so* full of herself. And she called Atlanta a small town. And she kept pronouncing my name wrong!" Shai complained to Emmie.

"Lots of people mispronounce your name," Emmie pointed out.

"No, not 'Shaianne.' '*Shai*.' She kept calling me 'Shane.'"

"That must have been super-annoying. Um, can we get back to page sixty-three now?"

The two friends were in Emmie's backyard,

preparing for their *Once on This Island* auditions. Emmie had decided to try out for the role of Erzulie, the Goddess of Love. And, of course, Shai still planned to try out for Ti Moune.

But now she had a problem— Grabby Gabby. Before, Shai had been 100 percent sure that she would be cast as Ti Moune. Now it was more like 50 percent. And 50 percent was *definitely* not as good as 100 percent.

"She should go for the part of the snobby rich girl, Andrea. That would be perfect for her," Shai murmured under her breath.

"Ahem! Page sixty-three. I want to run through Erzulie's song again. And Andrea isn't snobby. She's more like, you know, *sophisticated*."

"Maybe Gabby should be one of the gossipers, then. She seems like a gossipy person."

"Shai!"

"Okay, okay."

Shai turned her attention back to the script. Emmie cleared her throat. She pulled a pitch pipe out of her pocket and played an A note so that she would be in tune. Then she began singing "The Human Heart."

"The Human Heart" was a song about Ti Moune and Daniel, who liked each other. The problem was, Daniel was supposed to marry another girl—Andrea. Also, Ti Moune and

Daniel were from two different worlds. She was a peasant, and he came from a wealthy family.

"The courage of a dreamer," Emmie sang in her sweet, high voice.

There's that word again, Shai thought—"courage." The courage to be nice, the courage to dream. But wasn't courage about doing scary stuff? Like riding a bike for the first time? Like auditioning? Like trying to be okay with 50 percent sure versus 100 percent sure?

Now Emmie was singing about hopes that didn't come true.

Shai glanced at the music sheets and held up her hand. "You need to hold the word 'true' for eight counts, Em. You only did two counts."

Emmie groaned. "Oh, right! Ugh, I should have known that."

"It's okay. We've only had the music since Monday."

"Still. I can't forget these little details, or I won't get cast. My song needs to be perfect!"

Emmie repeated the line and tapped eight slow beats on her lap as she stretched out the word "true." Shai noticed that Emmie was pretty hard on herself about her singing. Emmie also was hard on herself about her cello playing and acting and every other subject they studied at their school.

Except for dancing. Shai noticed that whenever Emmie danced, she seemed happy and relaxed and lost in another world.

Of course, Shai could be hard on herself too. Like when she forgot one of her lines on the opening night of *Annie*. Or when she tripped on an oar during *The Princess and the Frog*. But for the most part, acting was her happiness and relaxation and escape.

Except when certain people were trying to steal certain roles away from her. . . .

Emmie ran through "The Human Heart" a few more times. She made a ton of notes in pencil in the margins of her script.

Then she and Shai switched places. Shai warmed up with some scales.

"Do-re-mi-fa-sol-la-ti-do!" she sang. "Do-re-mi-fa-so-done-with-this song!" she added as a joke.

"Ha-ha! Are you going to do 'Waiting for Life'? Or one of Ti Moune's other songs?" said Emmie.

Shai flipped through the music sheets. Ti Moune did have a lot of songs. When Aunt Mac-N-Cheese had played Ti Moune, she'd almost never left the stage. "Um . . . 'Waiting for Life,' I guess."

Shai felt stomach-achy all of a sudden and began to twist the music sheets in her hands. She didn't like thinking about how many songs Ti Moune had to sing. Ti Moune also had an important solo dance number.

Could Shai handle it all?

And to make things worse, Gabby wanted to be Ti Moune too. Normally Shai wouldn't have been worried about the competition. But Gabby was a professional. Plus, her unstructured improvisation scene had been well acted. *Strange,* sure, but well acted.

"Shai?"

"Hmm?"

"Why are you squeezing your music sheets into a pretzel?"

"What? Oops!"

Shai wondered if Penelope Periwinkle had a chapter called "Not Freaking Out."

SCENE 5

Break an Egg!

On Friday the backstage area of the school auditorium swarmed with students. Some were stretching, some were warming up their voices, and some were rehearsing their lyrics one last time.

As Shai waited for the auditions to start, she did her breathing exercises. She ran through a couple of tongue twisters to loosen up her mouth. She double-checked to make sure that she had worn her lucky not-matching

socks—one hearts sock and one stars sock. She had!

Nearby, Gabby paced back and forth. She was dressed in a peasant skirt and a ruffly top—the kind of outfit Ti Moune would wear.

Shai gulped. Should *she* have worn a Ti Moune outfit too? No one else had dressed as the character they were auditioning for. Still, maybe this was what professional actors did.

Panic, panic, panic.

"Ahhhhhh!" she breathed, trying to calm down. "Eeeeeee!"

And then she noticed Gabby reaching into her skirt pocket for something. It was a jar of what looked like honey.

Gabby unscrewed the top and sipped at it. Shai wrinkled her nose. Was this another Hollywood thing?

"Why are you drinking that?" Shai asked her.

Gabby rolled her eyes at Shai and kept pacing.

"Why is she drinking that?" Shai asked Rio, who was stretching his hamstrings.

"Singers do different stuff before they have to perform. Some of them drink herbal tea with honey to soothe their throats."

"Herbal tea? *Ew!*"

Rio grinned. "I always eat a banana before I go onstage. Nya does ten jumping jacks. Some people wear lucky underwear. Whatever works, right?"

Shai glanced down at her mismatched socks.
Hmm.

A few minutes later a fifth-grade helper-
person lined everyone up near the velvet curtain. "When Ms. Gremillion calls your name,
go out onto the stage and tell the
judges what you'll be singing,"
she said.

Shai found Emmie, and
they bustled into line
together. They were wrig-
gly with nervousness and
excitement, although at the
moment Shai felt more ner-
vous than excited. She ran a
hand over her sleeveless white
polka-dot dress. She touched her
sparkly headband. Why hadn't she
dressed more like Gabby?

"Break an egg!" Emmie said to Shai.

"Oh, yeah. Break an egg!" Shai said back to Emmie.

Actors were superstitious about saying "good luck" before a performance, so they always said "break a leg" instead. "Break an egg" was Shai and Emmie's own special version.

Emmie reached over and squeezed Shai's hand. Shai smiled, glad that her best friend was by her side.

"The courage to audition," Shai sang as a joke.

Emmie cracked up. Shai cracked up too.

"Rio Garcia, you're up first!" Ms. Gremillion called out from somewhere in the auditorium.

Rio squared his shoulders and sauntered onto the stage. He did a fancy twirl and bowed. After a moment he started singing a song called "Rain." His voice was strong and clear, and he even did some spiffy dance moves to go with the music.

Emmie went next and sang "The Human Heart." Shai put her fingers on her temples to send Emmie some positive vibes. Aunt Mac-N-Cheese had taught her about positive vibes, which were like magic brain waves combined with fairy dust.

The vibes worked really well, because Emmie sailed through her audition without a single mistake. When she walked off the stage, Shai gave her a double thumbs-up.

Gabby went after Emmie. Shai did *not* send her positive vibes.

Gabby began to sing "Waiting for Life." Shai gasped. That was *her* audition song. Was the girl out to steal *everything* from her?

"Wow, she's good!" Julia said from the back of the line. Several other kids nodded in agreement.

Shai's courage withered. Gabby *was* good. Really, *really* good. She had a beautiful voice that could be soft and whispery one measure and big and powerful the next. It was like a roller coaster of sounds and emotions.

When it was over, Gabby bowed and breezed off the stage. She passed by Shai and flashed a triumphant smile.

Shai's courage withered some more. How could she follow Gabby's act?

And then she remembered something else Grandma Rosa liked to say—"Always be positive!"

"Always be positive," Shai whispered to herself. Maybe saying the words would make them come true.

Someone was tugging at her arm.

"Shai? They're calling your name," Rio told her.

"What? Oh!"

Shai brushed past the velvet curtain and half-ran onto the stage. Along the way, she said a quick tongue twister under her breath: "Yellow leather, red feather. Yellow leather, red feather."

Shai went to the piece of white tape on the floor that marked center stage and blinked into the spotlight. She smiled at Ms. Gremillion and the two other people sitting in the front row— Ms. Englert, the dance teacher, and Mr. Martinez, the voice teacher.

"What will you be singing for us today, Shai?" Ms. Gremillion asked.

"Yellow leather, red feather— I mean, 'Waiting for Life.'"

"Great. Ready when you are."

Shai folded her hands and stared into the distance. She imagined that she was on a Caribbean island. She smelled the mangoes ripening on the trees. She felt the warm, tropical breeze on her face. She didn't think about Gabby at all.

When she was ready, she gave a little nod to the pianist, who also happened to be the music teacher, Mr. Yee. He played the introduction, and Shai started to sing.

"A stranger in white," she sang.

Right away Mr. Martinez made a face and wrote something on his clipboard. And not a nice face either, like, *That Shai Williams is so talented!* It was more of a cranky face, like, *That Shai Williams sounds like a croaky old frog!* Shai wondered, Had she come in too soon?

Or not soon enough? Or sung a D-sharp or a D-flat instead of a regular D? Shai was scared of Mr. Martinez, whose nickname was "Meany Martinez," and for good reason.

Don't freak out, Shai told herself. *Be positive.* At least Ms. Englert was beaming and bobbing her head to the music. Ms. Gremillion was watching and listening carefully, as she always did. Besides, Shai couldn't dwell on mistakes or maybe-mistakes. The show must go on. . . .

She focused on singing the rest of the song well. At the end she remembered to hold the last note for eleven long beats. Then she bowed and curtsied and bowed and curtsied again.

Shai practically danced off the stage. Except for Mr. Martinez's cranky face in the beginning, it had been a great audition—maybe even better than Gabby's.

Emmie rushed up to her and gave her a big,

squeezy hug. "You were amazetastic!"

"Thanks! You were amazetastic too."

The two girls sat down on an old theatrical trunk to watch the rest of the auditions. Shai peered over her shoulder to look for Gabby so that she could smirk at her.

But Gabby was surrounded by a group of kids. They were smiling at her and patting her on the shoulder.
Shai thought she
heard someone
say, "You'd be
an awesome
Ti Moune!"

No. Way. Had
they not just seen
her, Shai Williams,
deliver an A-plus-
plus audition?

Shai *ahhhhhhh*'d and *eeeeeee*'d some more to try to calm down. Sure, Gabby's audition had been okay. More than okay. But the teachers wouldn't pick Gabby for Ti Moune over Shai . . . would they?

After the last audition Shai and Emmie waited with everyone else while the teachers discussed and debated in secret. Who was going to be cast as whom?

After what seemed like forever, Ms. Gremillion came backstage, thanked everyone, and posted the cast list on the wall. The students gathered around eagerly.

Shai stood on tiptoes so that she could see over people's heads. Her heart was pounding like crazy. She saw that Emmie had been cast as Erzulie. *Yay, Emmie!* Rio had been cast as Agwe, the God of Water. *Go, Rio!*

But where was *her* name?

"Yesssss!" Gabby shouted.

Shai moved closer to the wall.

She saw:

TI MOUNE: GABBY SUPREME

MAMA EURALIE (TI MOUNE'S MOTHER):

SHAI WILLIAMS

Shai's heart sank all the way down to her lucky socks.

How could this have happened? Ti Mounc's *mother*? It was a nothing part. She could barely remember it from Aunt Mac-N-Cheese's production.

How could the teachers think Gabby would make a better Ti Moune?

Emmie came up to Shai and gave her another big, squeezy hug. "You totally should

have been Ti Moune," she said quietly.

"Thanks," Shai answered, trying to hold back her tears.

"I didn't eat my grapes from lunch. Do you want them?"

"Yup."

Grapes were Shai's number one comfort food.

Although right now she wasn't sure *anything* could comfort her.

SCENE 6

Lima Bean Sad Faces

"Jamal, please pass the mashed potatoes. Shai, sweetie, what's wrong with you tonight?" Momma asked her.

"Nothing," Shai mumbled. She could feel Sugar sniffing at her feet and waiting for magical falling crumbs.

"Nothing, huh? Is that why you made a sad face out of your lima beans?" Daddy asked, pointing to her plate.

"I'm ready for my Ooey-Gooey cake

now!" Samantha announced loudly.

"Sam, you have to eat your dinner before you have your dessert. Corn muffins aren't for throwing, mister!" Momma cried out as Jacobe stood up in his high chair and flung a corn muffin at Noodle. Noodle caught it in his mouth and scarfed it down in less than two seconds.

"That little man is going to be pitching for the Braves someday," Grandma Rosa said.

Grandma Rosa was Momma's momma. She lived around the corner in the house where she and Grandpa Lloyd had raised Momma, Aunt Mac-N-Cheese, and Uncle Milo. Grandma Rosa helped out a lot, especially with the younger kids, while Momma and Daddy were at work.

Grandpa Lloyd had passed away last year, and Shai still missed him every single day. She kept a picture of him on her dresser next to the glass bead bracelet he had bought for her in Italy, Europe.

The front door opened and closed. The dogs made bat ears and began barking like crazy. Aunt Mac-N-Cheese rushed into the dining room, smiling and breathless. She wore a pretty hat with feathers and flowers.

"Sorry I'm late, everyone! My rehearsal went over. And *of course* I had to pick up some yummy pecan candy for us to share later!"

She set a white box on the table and pulled up a chair next to Shai. "How'd your audition go today, Sweetpea?"

"Your audition!" Momma and Daddy said at the same time. "I put in the family calendar that it was *next* Friday. I'm so sorry, Shai," Momma added.

"It's okay," Shai replied. She knew how much stuff Momma had to keep track of— and Daddy, too. Besides, she had hoped she wouldn't have to talk about her audition at all tonight.

Of course Aunt Mac-N-Cheese had had to go and remember. Or maybe Ms. Englert had mentioned it to her. The two of them were friends from college.

"Is your audition the reason you're making lima bean sad faces?" Daddy asked her gently.

Shai picked up her fork and pushed the lima beans into a mini Mount Everest. "Uh-huh. Worst. Audition. Ever."

"Oh dear. What happened?" asked Grandma Rosa.

Shai shrugged. She had been asking herself the same thing. Would it have made a difference if she'd rehearsed more? Or worn a Ti Moune costume? Or done more Penelope Periwinkle exercises?

Or maybe the answer to Grandma Rosa's question was simple: *Gabby happened.*

"Someone else got Ti Moune. This new girl."

"Aww." Aunt Mac-N-Cheese reached over and hugged Shai. "That's rough. I'm sorry, Sweetpea."

Momma came over and hugged Shai too. So did Daddy and Grandma Rosa. Jamal gave her his corn muffin, with extra honey butter.

Samantha gave her five and a half lima beans. Jacobe made buzzy raspberry lips at her. This usually made her crack up, but tonight it only made her mouth twitch into a half smile.

"Did you guys know that *Once on This Island* has a lot in common with Hans Christian Andersen's story 'The Little Mermaid'?" Jamal spoke up. Shai's big brother knew something about everything.

"This boy is going to be a professor some-day," Grandma Rosa remarked.

"Definitely!" said Momma. "So, Shai, did you get another role?"

"Uh-huh. I have to play Ti Moune's mother," Shai groaned.

"Hey, that's wonderful!" said Daddy.

"It's the *opposite* of wonderful, Daddy. I was supposed to be Ti Moune, not Ti Moune's mother. Besides, mothers are old. And boring."

Momma chuckled. "Is that so?"

"Shaianne, have I told you about the time I did a play called *A Raisin in the Sun* on Broadway? My character was a mother, and she was *so* interesting," Grandma Rosa said.

Grandma Rosa used to be a famous stage actor. Aunt Mac-N-Cheese had followed in her path and studied drama in college. And now she, Shai, was carrying on the family's acting tradition. *Sort* of.

SHAI WILLIAMS STARS AS . . .

TI MOUNE'S MOM!

Blah.

"Do you know why they call it acting?" Grandma Rosa went on. "A good actor can *act* like someone she's not and make the audience *believe* she is that person." She paused dramatically.

"Are you up to that challenge, Shaianne Rosa Williams? Can you make your audience believe that you are Ti Moune's mother?"

Shai thought about this. Grandma Rosa was right.

"You have to eat your dinner before you have your dessert. Corn muffins aren't for throwing, mister!" Shai said in a pretend-Momma voice.

Samantha looked startled and spooned a bunch of lima beans into her mouth. Jacobe picked up his corn muffin and took a big, crumbly bite.

Hey, it works! Shai thought, surprised. She *was* a good actor.

"That's our girl," Grandma Rosa said, raising her glass of iced tea. Aunt Mac-N-Cheese raised her glass too. Momma and Daddy just laughed.

SCENE 7

Gabby Messes Up

On day one of rehearsals, Ms. Gremillion handed out copies of the rehearsal schedule. It said:

Once on This Island
Ms. Gremillion, Director
Mr. Martinez, Music Director
Ms. Englert, Choreographer

Week 1: Music (Monday-Friday)

Week 2: Choreography (Monday-Friday)

Week 3: Blocking and Scene Work (Monday-Friday)

Week 4: Full Run-Throughs (Monday–Thursday)

Week 4: Dress Rehearsal (Friday)

Week 4: Opening Night (Saturday)

Week 4: Closing Night (Sunday)

Shai and Emmie sat cross-legged on the stage and pored over the schedule together. It reminded them of last year's *Annie* schedule. That first week the cast had rehearsed the songs with Mr. Martinez's help. The second week Ms. Englert had taught them the dance steps. The third week Ms. Gremillion had shown them when, where, and how to move around on the stage. That third week they had also practiced their lines.

And finally, during the fourth week, they'd put it all together and run through the whole musical from beginning to end. On dress rehearsal night they'd done the run-through in full costume, hair, and makeup. Shai had loved the makeup part the best. As Miss Hannigan she'd gotten to wear red mean-lady lipstick and sparkly purple eye shadow!

Ms. Gremillion finished handing out the schedules. "Let me know if any of you have questions. Otherwise, please turn to page two of your scripts. Mr. Yee, can you give us an A-flat on the piano? Ruby and Isabella, eyes front. Jay, please get rid of that gum. Okay, let's get started. . . ."

For the next half hour the cast rehearsed

the opening number. A song called "We Dance" introduced the story and many of the main characters.

Then Mr. Martinez showed up and took over the rehearsal. Mr. Martinez was Very Serious about singing. He could also be a little scary—sometimes even super-scary. For example, there was the way he talked. It *sounded* like regular talking, but it *felt* like yelling. Shai and Emmie called it "quiet-yelling."

"You are singing in the wrong key!" Mr. Martinez quiet-yelled at Capone, who was playing Daniel.

"Eee-nun-cee-ate your words!" he quiet-yelled at Molly, who was playing Andrea.

Today the person he quiet-yelled at the most was Gabby.

"Why are you adding all those extra trills and slides? If the composer had intended

for them to be there, he would have written them in."

"But . . . I'm improvising," Gabby said with a confused expression.

"You cannot improvise in musical theater. You must sing the music exactly as it was written so that you can blend in with the rest of the cast."

"But Ti Moune is the most important character in the show. She needs to stand out!"

"Not in this scene. In this scene she is just one of the villagers. And you must stop thinking of Ti Moune as the most important character in the show. You are *all* important."

Gabby frowned and did an angry hair-flip.

Yay! Gabby is messing up! Shai thought.

Then she noticed something. Gabby's lower lip was quivering, as though she were about to start crying.

Oh.

It occurred to Shai that she should feel sorry for the girl. And a tiny, amoeba-size part of her did.

But mostly she was glad. Happy. Vindicated, which was one of Daddy's crossword puzzle words and meant, "Ha-ha! I was right!"

Shai really should have been Ti Moune.

SCENE 8

Practically a Star

Week two was dance rehearsals. On Monday after school, Ms. Englert gathered the cast onstage to teach them some choreography, a.k.a. dance steps, for one of the early scenes.

Ms. Englert was the opposite of Mr. Martinez. She was supersweet. She liked to tell silly jokes that were sometimes funny and sometimes not funny, but everyone laughed anyway. Last year for the *Annie* dress rehearsal, she had brought organic, sugar-free, smiley-face lollipops for the entire cast and crew.

Ti Moune's mother, Mama Euralie, wasn't in this particular scene, so Shai sat to the side and studied her lines. Every once in a while she looked up to check out the rehearsal.

Gabby seemed to be having a hard time with the choreography.

"Gabby, that's right, left, right," Ms. Englert called out with a helpful smile.

Gabby frowned and repeated the steps. She almost tripped on the last "right."

"Better! Now try it again and add the arms," said Ms. Englert.

Gabby repeated the steps a third time and flung her arms in the air. She looked like she was swatting at mosquitoes, which made Shai giggle.

"I don't get it," Gabby said, sounding frustrated.

Ms. Englert went up to Gabby and whispered something into her ear. Gabby nodded and walked over to where Shai was sitting.

Gabby flopped down with a heavy sigh. She reached into her backpack for her water bottle, which had an I ♥ SOCAL logo on it.

"Why aren't you rehearsing? And what's SoCal?" asked Shai.

"Southern California. Ms. Englert wants me to take a break. Whatever." She took a long sip of water and gazed moodily at the dancers on the stage. "Musicals are dumb."

"I thought you wanted to be in the show," Shai said, taken aback. *After all, you did kinda steal my part,* she wanted to add.

"I did. I do! But I've never been in a musical before, and it's totally not what I expected. It's so much work. Plus everyone's telling me what to do! It was different with the toothpaste commercial and with the zombie movie. I got to improvise a lot. With the toothpaste commercial, the director let me make up my *own* dance steps."

"Really?"

"Really. It was *way* better in Hollywood. I was practically a star, and no one ordered me around. Then we had to move here because of my dad's job. Now I'm stuck in this lame school

where no one appreciates *or* understands me!"

Shai was about to point out that the Sweet Auburn School was not a lame school. In fact, it was one of the best performing arts elementary schools in the country. Also, wasn't "practically a star" a little . . . dramatic?

But instead Shai said, "Do you know what Penelope Periwinkle would tell you right now?"

"Penelope who?"

"Chapter ten. A Great Actor must be able to adapt," Shai said in a fancy British accent. She had read on the book jacket that Penelope Periwinkle lived in England, Europe, and besides, Shai felt very smart, talking like that. "'Adapt' means changing yourself so that you can be the best you can be in a new environment or situation."

"I *know* what 'adapt' means," Gabby said,

sounding annoyed. "But shouldn't people adapt to me, too? Why do I have to do all the adapting? It isn't fair!"

Before Shai had a chance to answer, Ms. Englert waved to Gabby. "We're ready for you now!"

Gabby rolled her eyes and got to her feet.

Shai turned her attention back to her lines. It was hard to concentrate on them, though, because she was in a bad mood all of a sudden.

You know what's not fair? she wanted to say to Gabby. *You get to play Ti Moune, and you don't even appreciate it. I want to play Ti Moune more than anything else, and I don't get to. THAT'S not fair!*

As soon as the dance rehearsal was over, Shai grabbed her backpack, said bye to Emmie, and headed for the exit. Grandma Rosa would be waiting out front to walk her home.

"Shai?"

Shai turned around. It was Ms. Gremillion.

"Hi, Ms. Gremillion."

"Listen. Ms. Englert and I were just talking. We want to ask you something important. It's about the role of Ti Moune."

Shai's breath caught in her throat. Her heart did a crazy somersault. She knew exactly what Ms. Gremillion was going to say next.

We made a mistake casting Gabby as Ti Moune. Would you be willing to play Ti Moune instead?

"I'll do it!" Shai announced. Her feet started happy-dancing.

"You will?"

"Yes!"

Shai hoped Gabby wouldn't be too upset about being replaced. Although maybe she would be relieved? She'd sounded pretty miserable earlier.

"That's great, but . . . let me explain first,"

Ms. Gremillion said. "Ms. Englert and I would love it if you could help Gabby. This is her first stage show, and we think she could use some support from someone with lots of stage experience—like you."

Shai stared at her.

Help Gabby? The one who stole the role away from me? The one who doesn't even want to be in the show?

"Shai?" Ms. Gremillion was waiting for her to say something.

"Yeah. I'll do it," Shai repeated. But this time her feet weren't happy-dancing.

Not one bit.

SCENE 9

Taking the High Road

Shai sat at the kitchen table working on her character journal. Next to her was an array of excellent snacks: beef jerky, gummy worms, and her favorite blue power drink. Sugar was a warm, snoring puddle at her feet.

Today had been the last day of dance rehearsals with Ms. Englert. On

Monday they would begin blocking and scene work with Ms. Gremillion.

After her conversation with Ms. Gremillion, Shai had come around to the idea of helping Gabby. Sort of. Kind of. After all, Ms. Gremillion had asked her, and how could Shai let her teacher down?

She'd discussed it with Momma and Daddy too, and they'd described something called "taking the high road," which meant being mature and adaptable.

So Shai had taken the high road. She'd tried about a billion zillion times to give Gabby advice about Ti Moune. But each time, Gabby had either ignored her or said something mean and snarky. Like: "I'm sorry, were *you* in a Hollywood movie?" Or: "What do *you* know about being a star?"

Now Shai turned her attention back to the

character journal. She needed to forget about Gabby and high roads for a while and focus on her own role. She wanted to make sure she understood Mama Euralie's character really well so that she could say her lines in a convincing way.

According to Penelope Periwinkle, a character journal was a useful tool for this. It was basically a notebook filled with information about your character. Where did she live? Who were her friends and family? What was her favorite herbivore dinosaur? Stuff like that.

Shai dangled a gummy worm into her mouth. Then she picked up her turquoise marker and wrote:

CHARACTER: MAMA EURALIE
• She and Tonton Julian found little Ti

Moune in a magical tree and raised
her as their daughter.

- Ti Moune grows up, saves Daniel
from his car accident, and falls
in love with him. She wants to go
to the other side of the island to
be with him, but Mama Euralie
and Tonton Julian try to stop
her. Ti Moune is just a peasant,
and Daniel and his family are
grands hommes (that means big,
important people). Mama Euralie
and Tonton Julian are worried
that the grands hommes will
reject Ti Moune and be super-
mean to her.

- Mama Euralie wants to take care of
Ti Moune. She doesn't want her to
get hurt.

Shai considered this for a moment. Her brain began to improvise.

She flipped to a fresh page and wrote:

CHARACTER: GABBY SUPREME
- She and her family just moved to Atlanta from Hollywood.
- She was in a toothpaste commercial. She was in a zombie potato movie, too.
- She doesn't want to be here.
- She wants to do everything her own way.
- She thinks no one appreciates or understands her.

The kitchen door opened. Momma walked in carrying the mail, a cardboard box, and a canvas bag full of vegetables. Sugar trotted up to her and sniffed at her ankles.

"Hi, Shai. Where is everybody?" Momma asked as she unloaded everything onto the counter.

"Upstairs with Grandma Rosa. She's teaching Jamal and Samantha how to play chess, and Jacobe's taking a nap. Is my tongue blue?"

Momma laughed. "Uh-huh."

Sugar started barking at the cardboard box.

"What is the matter with you?" Shai asked Sugar.

Momma bent down and spoke softly to the box. Then she reached inside and pulled out a cat. It had scruffy gray fur and a bunch of missing teeth. Its golden eyes looked frightened.

Sugar barked at the cat. The cat hissed at Sugar.

"She's a stray," said Momma. "No one seems to want her because she can be a bit . . . well, cranky. But she's probably a sweetheart, deep

down. I thought we might give her a home for a while, until she sorts things out."

Shai knew what that meant. Momma had said those same words when she'd brought home Patches and Noodle and Furball and Purrball and all their other animals.

"Hey, kitty," Shai said, reaching out her hand.

The cat hissed and swiped at Shai with her claws.

"These things take time," Momma said to Shai. She snuggled the cat to her chest. The cat hissed at her but didn't try to escape. "Come on, Crabbycakes. Let's get you into a quiet room so you can do some cat yoga and chill out."

Shai glanced down at her character journal.

Her brain began to improvise again. Maybe Gabby was like the new cat. Maybe she was cranky on the outside but sweet on the inside. Maybe she just needed someone to appreciate and understand her.

Maybe Shai shouldn't give up on her just yet.

"Momma?"

"Hmm?"

"Can I use the phone to call a friend from school?"

"*May* I. And yes, you may."

Shai found Gabby's family's phone number on the rehearsal carpool list. Then she punched in the number.

It was Gabby who answered. "Hello?"

"Hey, Gabby? It's Shai Williams."

There was a long silence.

"Gabby, are you there?"

"What do you want?"

Shai tried to think of her next line. How could she make Gabby feel appreciated and understood?

And then it came to her. *She* would ask *Gabby* for help.

"Hey, so . . . I need some advice about those scenes with Ti Moune and Mama Euralie. Do you want to meet at the Scoop, maybe tomor-

row afternoon? Like three o'clock?" Shai asked.

There was another long silence.

"Sweets and Treats has better ice cream," Gabby said finally.

Shai stuck her tongue out at the phone.

"Shai? Are you there?"

"Yup! Sweets and Treats.

Tomorrow at three. I'll be there. Bye!"

Shai hung up.

"Was that the new girl? The one you tried to help before?" Momma called out over her shoulder.

"Yup!"

Momma smiled. "You're a good egg, Shai Williams. That was a very kind thing to do. Very high road."

Shai smiled back. "Does that mean I get to play extra video games tonight?"

"We'll see. Love you, sweetie."

"Love you too, Momma."

Shai returned to the kitchen table to work on her character journal. Just yesterday she'd remembered to ask Grandma Rosa about that saying, "Have the courage to be nice to people."

"It takes courage to be nice to folks who aren't always nice to you," Grandma Rosa had replied.

Shai finally got that. It had been a little scary, being nice to Gabby just now.

Hopefully, it would be worth it.

And hopefully, Gabby would have the courage to be nice back . . . at least a little.

SCENE 10

The Gummy Bear Triangle

Sweets and Treats was busy on Saturday afternoon. When Shai and Emmie got there, they found Gabby waiting in a corner booth.

"What's *she* doing here?" were the first words out of Gabby's mouth as she scowled at Emmie. "I thought we were going to work on Ti Moune and Mama Euralie's scenes."

So much for nice, Shai thought, disappointed. "Emmie wanted to ask you for some acting advice too," she improvised quickly.

She elbowed Emmie. Emmie elbowed her back. The truth was, Shai needed her best friend beside her for moral support. She wasn't sure she could handle a whole hour of Crabby Grabby Gabby all by herself.

Shai and Emmie slid into the booth across from Gabby. Daddy and Jacobe were seated at a nearby table with coloring books and crayons. They had walked Shai and Emmie to Sweets and Treats.

The waiter came by to take the girls' orders. Shai ordered strawberry ice cream with whipped cream and gummy bears. Emmie ordered the same thing with peach ice cream. Gabby ordered a "lemon froyo." Shai figured out that "froyo" was Hollywood language for "frozen yogurt."

"So, Gabby, . . . I need your advice. What do you think I should do with Mama Euralie's

character? I can't quite figure her out," Shai said. Which wasn't 100 percent the truth, or even 50 percent the truth, since she had done the character journal and all—but Gabby didn't know that.

"Well, Mama Euralie is a mom. *Obviously*," Gabby said with a hair-flip. "And most moms worry about their daughters, right? So Mama Euralie worries about Ti Moune. She doesn't want Ti Moune to go to the other side of the island. She doesn't want her to get her heart broken or be treated badly by people or put herself in danger."

Shai already knew all this, but she nodded and acted as though she didn't. "Huh. That's really, really interesting! So do you think Ti Moune feels bad about not listening to her mom?"

"Well, yes and no. Ti Moune loves her mom.

But she's independent; she wants to do things her own way," Gabby replied. "Again, *obviously*."

The ice cream and froyo arrived, and the girls dug in.

"You know what?" Emmie said through a mouthful of peach ice cream. "Our three characters are like a triangle!" She took three gummy bears and formed a triangle on her napkin. "Ti Moune is at the top of the triangle. She's super-independent. And here's Erzulie. She's the Goddess of Love, so she understands that Ti Moune wants to be with the boy she loves, even if it's dangerous or whatever. And here's Mama Euralie, who wants to protect Ti Moune."

Gabby laughed. "I like that! We're a gummy bear triangle!"

Shai sat up. A smile tugged at her lips. She had never heard Gabby laugh in a happy way. This was a small victory.

"Hey, new topic! What do you guys think of Ms. Englert's choreography?" asked Shai. She looked right at Emmie when she said this and sent her an ESP mind-reading message: *This is unstructured improvisation! Pretend the choreography is hard!*

"It's *so* hard," Emmie replied immediately. "I wish we had more dance rehearsals! But next week is blocking and scene work."

Great improvising! Shai thought. "Hey, do you guys want to come over to my house tomorrow? Our living room is perfect for practicing dance steps," she said out loud.

"That's an amazetastic idea!" said Emmie. "What about you, Gabby?"

"No, thanks," said Gabby. She picked up the Ti Moune gummy bear, studied it, and set it down again. "Well, maybe. Yeah, all right. I don't have anything better to do, I guess."

Under the table Shai gave Emmie a double thumbs-up sign. Another small victory! At this rate Gabby would have a total personality change and become as sweet as ice cream in no time.

Or maybe froyo.

Or maybe Shai was getting ahead of herself.

SCENE 11

Curtain!

The three girls met several times a week to rehearse on their own before opening night. Ms. Gremillion told Shai that she was really pleased with Gabby's progress.

When opening night finally arrived, Shai, Emmie, Gabby, and the rest of the cast were ready.

Well, *kind* of ready.

Half an hour before curtain, the backstage was complete and total chaos. "Curtain" was theater language for when the show was due to start.

"I can't find my head thingamabob-ber!" someone shouted.

"I forgot my vest!" someone else shouted.

"Has anyone seen the sewing kit?"

"I can't remember any of my lines!"

"I think I'm going to throw up!"

Shai sat very still on a wooden crate while one of the parent-helpers, Sarah Swanson's mom, did her hair and makeup. People swirled around them—arranging the set pieces, searching for missing stuff, double-checking everything. Rio was eating a banana. Nya was doing jumping jacks. Gabby was pacing and drinking honey.

The stage had been transformed into a beautiful tropical village. A construction-paper tree and a ladder and towered in the background. Fake vines hung from the rafters. Hand-painted flowers sprouted from the wooden floorboards.

Mrs. Swanson uncapped a makeup crayon. "Just a few more worry lines on your forehead, Shai, and . . . Voilà! You look just like a stressed-out mom. Here, check it out."

Shai gazed at her reflection in the mirror. Thick creams and powders caked her face. Stage makeup was heavier than regular makeup, since the audience had to see it all the way from their seats. A rainbow-colored scarf covered her hair.

"Thank you, Mrs. Swanson!"

"You're welcome, honey. All righty, who's next? Ezra, you're up. Let's transform you into Papa Ge! I just need to find my sly demon makeup...."

Shai got up from the crate and walked over to the velvet curtain. Her silk skirt made swishy noises as she moved. She touched her head covering and then her lucky not-matching socks, which were in her pockets because of the everyone-has-to-go-barefoot costume rule.

She had considered trading them in for new lucky socks, but had decided at the last minute to give them another chance.

Besides, she wasn't "sangry"—sad and angry—anymore about having to play Mama Euralie.

On the other side of the closed curtain, the orchestra warmed up and the audience buzzed and whispered. The scene reminded Shai of opening night last year, and the year before, and the years before that, all the way back to when she'd played a busy ladybug in preschool. Opening nights always made her palms sweaty and her stomach churny and her heart thumpy-racy. She remembered, though, that as soon as the curtain went up, her palms and stomach and heart would grow suddenly calm. Something deep inside her knew exactly what to do. Her brain and body stopped being Shai for a while and became her character one billion zillion percent.

Shai's fingers searched for an opening in the curtain and found one. She peeked through ... and there was her family! Momma, Daddy, Grandma Rosa, Aunt Mac-N-Cheese, Jamal ... even Jacobe was there, wearing his dinosaur pj's so he could fall asleep in his stroller later. Samantha was moving her lips and pretending to read the program.

Shai let the curtain drop shut. Nearby she saw Emmie singing softly to herself. She looked very Goddess-of-Love in her crimson dress and pink flower wreath.

"Break an egg," Shai said, joining her.

"Break an egg!" Emmie replied.

Gabby overheard them. "Um, guys? It's s posed to be 'break a *leg*.'"

"'Break an egg' is better," Emmie told her.

Shai nodded. *"Way* better. It's a super-secret good-luck phrase. Only two people in the universe know about it. Well, three, now."

Gabby considered this. "Huh."

"Break an egg, Gabby. And don't forget what we talked about for Ti Moune's last scene. When she turns into the magical tree? Stand with your arms stretched out like this," Shai said, posing.

"Right. Thanks," Gabby said. She resumed her pacing and honey-drinking.

In the last couple of weeks, Gabby had been a wee bit nicer. She had started to act more comfortable and confident in her Ti Moune role too. Shai liked to think that she and Emmie had helped her with that. At yesterday's dress rehearsal Gabby had gotten all her dance steps right. She'd sung the songs without adding extra notes. She'd delivered her lines in a really convincing way.

"Has anyone seen my top hat?" someone yelled.

"I just spilled grape juice on my shirt!"

"We need more blue face paint!"

"Where are the safety pins?"

"This microphone isn't working!"

And then it was curtain time! Ms. Gremillion asked the cast to gather around her. Mr. Martinez and Ms. Englert showed up too, as did the fifth-grade crew members who were in charge of the sound and lights and sets.

"You guys have worked hard these past four weeks. I'm very proud of each and every one of you," Ms. Gremillion said. "Now the hard work is over, and it's time to go out there and have some fun!"

Everyone held hands and gave a loud cheer.

Then they all took their places. The stage went dark except for a few dim pools of light. The orchestra began to play, and the cymbals made thunder sounds. A hush fell over the audience.

Shai's palms and stomach and heart grew

calm. Her brain and body became Mama
Euralie one billion zillion percent.

The curtain went up. The

Storytellers and the Gods spoke their first lines.

Then the cast burst into song.

The Cast Party (with Extra Cheese and Pepperoni)

That night everyone showed up for the cast party at Shai's dad's pizza restaurant.

The opening night performance had been amazetastic! There had been a few tiny problems, like Ruby, Isabella, and Glenn missing their cues, and Capone tripping in the ballroom scene and knocking down a couple of set pieces. But overall the entire cast and crew had done an incredible job. Even Mr. Martinez had clapped at the end and sort of smiled in his squinchy, head-tilty way.

Shai had gotten lots of applause as Mama Euralie. And that hadn't even been the best part! The best part had been when the whole cast had taken a bow together, and the audience had given them a standing ovation.

"We are so proud of you," Momma said, hugging Shai for the billionth zillionth time.

"I couldn't have played

Mama Euralie better myself," Grandma Rosa chimed in.

"Same!" Aunt Mac-N-Cheese agreed.

"*I* could've," Samantha said, which made everyone laugh, although Shai knew that her little sister wasn't joking. "Can I have a piece of the congraduation cake yet? I'm done with my dinner. I ate one and one-quarter triangles of pizza!"

Later Shai and Emmie went around the restaurant with trays to help pass out seconds of pizza. Shai spotted Jamal hanging out at a corner table with some of his friends from middle school. Jacobe was playing inside tag with Emmie's twin brothers; all three boys were covered with tomato sauce.

Shai and Emmie stopped at Rio and Garrett's table. The boys were in their regular clothes, but their faces were still smudged with makeup, which was pretty much how the rest of the cast looked.

"Good job, Rio!" Shai said as she put another slice of pizza on his plate. "You too, Garrett. Hey, Rio. Are your parents here? I haven't seen them."

Rio fidgeted. "Actually, they both had to work tonight, so . . ." His eyes lit up. "Hey! Who's got the present for Ms. Gremillion? Wasn't Nya in charge of it? We should give it to Ms. Gremillion when we cut the cake, right?"

Rio and Garrett began discussing the present, which was a T-shirt with the words WORLD'S BEST DIRECTOR on it.

Shai and Emmie moved on. At the next table Gabby was holding court with a bunch of people.

"—and when you gave up your life for Daniel's and morphed into a magical tree, I just cried and cried," somebody's mom was saying to her.

"Oh, thank you! Did you like the way I posed when I turned into the tree?" Gabby stood up and held out her arms. "That was my idea!"

Shai made an O mouth at Emmie. Emmie O-mouthed back. *Shai* had come up with the tree pose idea and had convinced Gabby to do it.

Gabby waved to Shai and Emmie as she approached them.

"Good job, guys!" Gabby said.

"You too, Gabby," said Shai.

"You were really good," Emmie added.

Gabby regarded them. She had sparkly green eye shadow on her eyelids and magenta blush on her cheeks.

"Yeah. So. I wanted to, um . . . That is, I should probably say thank you for . . ." Gabby's gaze dropped to the floor. "What I mean is, thanks for letting me help you guys out. With your acting and stuff. And I guess you kind of helped me, too, so thanks," she blurted out.

"No problem," said Shai.

"Yeah, you're welcome," Emmie added.

A sweet, comfortable silence settled among them. Then Gabby glanced at the trays Shai and Emmie were carrying. "Hey, why are you hogging all the pizza?" she demanded suddenly.

Crabby Grabby Gabby is back! Shai thought.

"What kind do you want? Pepperoni or extra cheese?" asked Shai.

"Well, pepperoni, *obviously*. Extra cheese is boring."

Extra cheese was Shai's favorite. "No, it's not!"

"Yes, it is!"

"No, it's not!"

"Yes, it is!"

Emmie held up her hands. "Hey, guys? Why don't we just sit down and eat? Then we can decide."

"Fine."

"Fine."

The three girls sat down and dug into their pizza.

It was an almost-perfect ending to an almost-perfect opening night.